The Erl King's
Daughter

This edition first published in Great Britain in 1999
First published in Great Britain 1988 by Mammoth
an imprint of Egmont Children's Books Limited
239 Kensington High Street, London W8 6SA
Published in hardback by Heinemann Library,
a division of Reed Educational and Professional Publishing Limited
by arrangement with Egmont Children's Books Limited.
Text copyright © Joan Aiken 1988
Illustrations copyright © Paul Warren 1988
Additional Illustrations copyright © 1999
The Author and Illustrator have asserted their moral rights.
Paperback ISBN 0 7497 3580 5
Hardback ISBN 0 431 06191 2
10 9 8 7 6 5 4 3 2 1
A CIP catalogue record for this title
is available from the British Library.
Printed at Oriental Press Limited, Dubai.

JOAN AIKEN

The Erl King's Daughter

Illustrated by Paul Warren

 YELLOW BANANAS

Chapter One

THESE THINGS HAPPENED to my younger brother Kevin when I had my busted leg. If I hadn't been in hospital, maybe I could have helped him.

While I was away from home, Aunt Ada came to look after Kev – and Aunt Ada's no more use than last week's paper. She's thin, and forgets everything you tell her; she has a whiny voice and a drip on her nose. And does embroidery.

Well. Just after I got my leg busted, a new girl, Nora Scull, turned up in Kev's class at our school, that's Kimballs Green Junior. Kev told me about her.

Kev's good at telling stories. He got the knack from our gran. Gran came from abroad when she was little, with *her* gran, who knew endless tales about trolls and kobolds and witches. Our gran passed them to Kev, and he told them to the kids at school.

Kev is little and pale and scrawny. He can't
run fast, for he gets breathless, so he does more
watching and thinking than other people. He
knows lots of words. He reads all the labels on
packets, and tells stories better than I can; I
always seem to get the end bits at the
beginning, or forget the middle.

When he came to see me at Squire's Park Hospital, Kev told me about this Nora. She was in his class, though she was older, because she never had much schooling; her dad was always moving house. She was skinny as a broom, Kev said, with eyes black as lumps of soot, and a sharp nose. Her hair was dark and thick, so bushy that she always seemed to be hidden behind it, in a dark corner of her own. She never laughed, never smiled. Just watched all the time. Rather like Kev, in a way.

Right from the start, Nora took a fancy to Kev. He couldn't say why. She

was older and bigger, you'd think she'd want to
be with those her own age. But no. Maybe it
was because of Kev's tales. Though, he said, if
he did tell one, she'd sneer at it, and say it was a
silly baby story.

Only one she really liked. That was the tale of the Erl King. It was one our gran told, about the land *her* gran came from, where there's miles of forest. In those big woods there lives a spook, his name's the Erl King. He rides at

night, on his black horse that's fast as the wind,
but quiet.

And there was a farmer who had to go through the woods one night, taking his sick kid to the doctor.

The man carries the kid on his back, and it keeps crying, saying, 'Dada, Dada, the Erl King's after us, he's grabbing at me with his cold hands.'

Well, the father runs faster and faster, but it's no use.

When he gets to the doctor's house, the little
kid is stone-cold dead in his carry-bag.

The Erl King had got him.

When Kev told the story to kids at school, he
changed it. Instead of those foreign woods, he
had the father running along the footpath that's
the disused railway between Turnpike Heath
and Squire's Park Hospital. There's a patch of
copse on Turnpike Heath, runs down to the
railway cutting. After Kev told the story, some
kids wouldn't go near those woods, or the
railway path. They said the Erl King would
get them.

Nora really dug that story, Kev said. After
she'd made him tell it once or
twice, *she* got to telling it,
and made it more scary
each time, putting in
awful things.

'Do you *like* Nora?' I asked Kev, when he
came to see me in hospital.

'No,' he said. 'No, I don't like her.'

I found out later he'd stopped telling stories
himself. As if they'd begun to frighten him.

Chapter Two

WHEN AUNT ADA brought Kev visiting I could
see there was something wrong, for he'd got so
thin and waxy-pale, with eyes big as olives and
dark hollows under them. But then I thought it
was from grieving for our gran, who'd died not
long before. Kev and Gran were very close.
Besides telling him tales, she'd let him help her
about the house, before he started school.
They'd chatter to each other all day, about
anything from people to potatoes. So it was to
be expected he'd miss her badly.

Gran was a great cook. Not fancy – she'd no time or cash for that – but things you don't get in other kids' homes: onion-and-raw potato pancakes, gingerbread, cheese pudding, home-baked beans. After Aunt Ada came, it was all frozen stuff. 'I'm no cook, never have been,' she'd sniff. 'Can't expect me to cook as well as take care of two children. All that trouble at my age.' It was fish fingers and peas, day after day, Kev told me.

And do you know what Aunt Ada *did*? She got rid of all Gran's things. Every bit. Her clothes went to the jumble; and her brass pot and meat-pounder, her curved chopper, wooden spoons and big wooden bowl were sold to Mr Simms, who has the secondhand shop on Turnpike Hill.

Worst of all for Kev, he found that her little cookery book had gone too. It wasn't much bigger than a packet of raisins, with a greasy cover and a thick old rubber band round, because of all the bits that were tucked into it. Gran had it from her gran, and both of them had written in the margins, and drawn little pictures (to show how things ought to be cut or peeled or shaped). They had stuck in clips from newspapers and magazines, and written translations of the foreign words, till it was more like a family scrap-album than a cookery book.

When Kev got home from school and found the book gone from the salt-and-pepper shelf, he was really upset.

'I disposed of it,' Aunt Ada says when he asked her. 'Best you got nothing to remind you of your gran. You fret too much as it is.'

Kev did go and ask Mr Simms about it, but the book wasn't sold to him. And Kev couldn't find it in the dustbin either.

That was a bad time for him, and the new girl, Nora Scull, she made things worse.

She was always following Kev. 'Softy,' she called him, or 'Dummy.'

One day he saw Miss Clamp's brooch in the playground and picked it up. Nora snatched it.

'You give me that, Softy!'

'It's Miss Clamp's!'

'Give it here!'

'It's not yours.'

'Give it, or I'll put such an ache in your head you can't see the blackboard.'

Kev gets these awful headaches sometimes. He has to go home and lie down. Nora knew about them.

'I can give you one,' she told him. 'If I point my finger – like this!'

Just the sight of that skinny pointing finger, and her dark eyes, like black holes, made Kev's head begin to throb.

'Do you know who I *am*?' she says.

'You're Nora Scull.'

'I'm the Erl King's daughter. If you don't do what I say, my dad'll come and fetch you.'

Chapter Three

WELL – KEV BELIEVED Nora. Where she
lived, down Spital Way, that's a very bad
neighbourhood. Kimballs Green is a poor part
of London, and Spital Way, in the middle, is the
worst bit. Nora lived in a squat, with her father.
It was a derelict house, all boarded up. Nora
climbed in through a hole over a rusty tank.
She tried to get Kev to go in, but he wouldn't.
It was just the kind of place, he thought, where
the Erl King would choose to live, with rusty
cookers and smashed TV sets in the front yard.

'Don't you tell the others about my dad,' says
Nora. 'I'll know if you do. I know all that
happens to you. If you tell, my dad will get
you, on his black Koniyashi, what can go
upstairs and in windows.'

So when Miss Clamp asked in Assembly, had anyone seen her brooch, he kept quiet. He felt awful about it though, because he liked Miss Clamp.

None of the other kids could stand Nora, so, as Nora was always with Kev, his friends stopped talking to him. She'd follow him home. Aunt Ada didn't mind Nora. 'I don't object to a quiet, well-behaved child,' she said. Nora would sit in our front room, with her sharp eyes everywhere, waiting for a chance to nip a chocolate biscuit, or a 20p from Aunt Ada's purse. She never took enough to notice, but she was always thieving.

'If you tell, I'll say you took it,' she told Kev.

Chapter Four

THERE'S AN OLD blind man, sits on a box
outside Kimballs Green tube station. Mr
Greenway, his name is. He has his dog, Spot,
on his lap, and a plate in front for coins people
drop in. He doesn't get much. And Spot always
looks a bit embarrassed, sitting on Mr
Greenway's lap like that. He's too big, and his
legs hang down. Still, he puts up with it. He
gives his stumpy tail a wag when Kev goes by,
because sometimes Kev brings him a bone.

One day, walking past the station – 'Wouldn't it
be a lark to tip Spot into the road?' says Nora.

'No it *wouldn't*,' says Kev.

But, without listening, Nora gives Mr
Greenway a hard shove; over he goes, on the
pavement, and Spot is thrown clear into the
traffic. There's a
screech of brakes.

Next, Nora's picking
Mr Greenway up, making a big fuss.
'Oh, you poor man! I saw
those wicked boys knock you over!'
Butter wouldn't melt in her mouth. While she

was setting him back on his box, she half-inched 50p from his money.

Spot came limping out of the traffic. 'Lucky he wasn't killed,' said an angry motor-cyclist.

'I'm not going to talk to you any more,' says Kev to Nora. 'That was a horrible, horrible trick to play.'

'If you tell, I'll strike you blind,' says Nora. 'How'd you like to sit on a box for the rest of your life, in the dark? I can do it,' she says, 'if I point my finger at you.'

And Kev believed her. When she pointed her finger, everything he could see began to darken and blur.

Then Nora made him go into shops and ask for things that were hard to find – junket mix, or almond flavouring – and while the shopkeeper was hunting, she'd whip something from near the door, chewing-gum or all-sorts. If the shopkeeper found some junket mix she'd say, 'No, that's not the sort Mum wants.'

Kev was growing even thinner. He had awful dreams at night, about the Erl King coming to shut him up in the dark for ever. And his headaches got worse.

I worried about him, but my leg hadn't mended, I was still in hospital. What could I do?

Chapter Five

ONE DAY NORA says to Kev, 'Come on, I've found a crummy old bookshop in March Street, run by an old girl who's deaf as a post; we can sneak up behind her and take all the cash out of her drawer.'

Kev didn't want to. He hated that part of Kimballs Green, where Nora lived. He was afraid Nora's father might come out of the Squat and get him.

'I won't come,' he said.

'I'll make your head ache,' says Nora. 'You'll go blind!' And she points her finger. Right away, he can feel a thumping start, behind his eyes.

So he went with Nora, but very slowly, lagging behind, thinking about Gran. If only Gran was still here, he thought. *She* wouldn't put up with Nora. 'I don't like folk that's out only for themselves,' she used to say. 'That sort, you want to have nothing to do with them. Tell them to clear out.' 'But what if they won't clear off, Gran?' Kev asked her once.

And what had Gran said?

'Here's the place,' Nora said, in a dingy street that led off Spital Way. The house doors opened flat on the pavement. Most were boarded up. But one was still open, and the window was full of grimy books.

It was a foggy October evening, cold, starting to get dark.

Kev could
just see, through the
grubby window, shelves round the
small shop, full of books, and a desk in the
middle, with more books piled up, and
somebody sitting behind them. Kev had never
seen a shop full of books before – there's none
where we live, top of Squire's Hill – and he
couldn't help being interested, in spite of
feeling so sick and scared.

But Nora seemed annoyed. A grey sour look

went over her face – like the
wind shifting over a bed of
nettles. 'There's someone
new,' she says sharply.
'Maybe the old lady died.
We must think of another
plan. I know: you go in.
Start looking around. I'll stay
outside, and soon I'll shout Help! Help!
The chap will run out, to see what's
happening, and you grab the money.
It's in a green tin cashbox. Go on – hurry up.'

So Kev went into the shop – scared, not
wanting to, yet keen to see this place full of
books.

And another part of him was thinking about
Spital Way, just round the corner, where Nora's
father, the Erl King, lived in his dark Squat; and
another part was trying to remember what Gran
had said – what *had* she said – about bad
people, and how to deal with them?

Something about dark, it was.

If only he could remember.

He went into the shop, which smelled of old, dusty books. The young man at the desk glanced up from a paper he was holding and gave him a half smile.

'Hallo. Looking for any book in particular?'

Kev could only mumble. 'Can I – can I look round?'

'Feel free.'

The young fellow – he was pale, with ginger hair – went back to his reading. Outside the window, Kev could see Nora's eyes like two black holes looking in.

Kev stared at all the books – there were thousands, hardbacks and paperbacks. How long would it take to read them? Weeks, months. Then he looked back at Nora. She was pointing towards the desk drawer. Kev moved a little closer to it.

Then his eyes nearly dropped out of his head. Open on the desk, with all its bits spread about, and its thick rubber band, was Gran's cookery book. *That* was what the man was studying so carefully!

'Why!' said Kev. 'That's my gran's cookbook! That's her book! Did – did Aunt Ada sell it to you?'

'Not to me,' says the young man. 'I just took over this place. Was your gran called Martha Green?'

'Yes – *yes* – and all those notes are in her writing – and my great-gran's –'

Kev was trembling. Partly, because he had just begun to remember what Gran had said – about dark.

'It's the most wonderful book!' The man was saying. 'I'm going to try and get it published – notes and all – did your gran draw those pictures?'

'Yes, she did –'

'I'm sure I can find a publisher who'll do it –'

Now Kev remembered exactly what Gran had said. '*Let them go*,' Gran had said. 'Bad people have their own dark inside them. Just you keep clear of them,

Kev, my boy. Let them go, and they'll get lost in the dark.'

Kev thought of the Erl King, riding through the dark on his motorbike, with his long bony fingers reaching out, ready to grab. He thought of the black holes of Nora's eyes.

And, just at that moment, he heard Nora's voice outside.

'Help! *Help*! HELP!'

'Save us, what's that?' gasped the man. He jumped out and rushed to the door. Forgetting the cashbox, Kev followed into the street.

Now – here's the queer part.

That street was entirely empty, from end to end.

Not a soul to be seen. Nora wasn't there. They found nobody, though they hunted from end to end of March Street, from Squire's Hill to Kimballs Green tube.

Chapter Six

NORA WASN'T AT school next day, in her seat next to Kev. He never saw her again. In November, a demolition team knocked down the whole row of houses in Spital Way, where the Erl King had his Squat.

Quite a few kids at Kimballs Green Junior aren't certain if Nora was ever there.

When my leg finally mended, I came out of hospital, and, after a while, Kev began to look better.

The bookshop man – Alan Hudnut's his name – has found a publisher who'll print Gran's book. *The Survivors' Kitchen Book*, it'll be called. They'll print all Gran's little pictures, and what she wrote in the front: 'This book is for my grandson Kevin Green.' Alan thinks Kevin might get quite a bit of money from it.

Aunt Ada is still thin and whiny, but Kev and I do the cooking now, so she just sits in the front room and embroiders. (She only got 15p from Alan's Auntie Tilly for the book. It was hardly worth walking all that way down Squire's Hill.)

Kev's going to be a famous chef when he's older. He has lost interest in telling stories.

But the queer thing is that the kids at school *still* tell the story of the Erl King; and lots of them won't go along the old railway path to Squire's Park, or into Turnpike Woods. They say the woods are haunted by a witch girl called Nora Scull.

The End

Yellow Bananas are bright, funny, brilliantly imaginative stories written by some of today's top writers. All the books are beautifully illustrated in full colour.

So if you've enjoyed this story, why not pick another from the bunch?

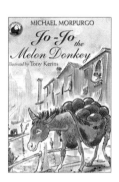